the BAD GUYS

in

ATTACK OF THE ZITTENS

· AARON BLABEY ·

the BAD GUYS

in

SCHOLASTIC INC.

ATTACK OF THE ZITTENS

(GOOD)

ZOMBIE KITTEN INVASION!

ATTACK OF THE ZITTENS

Good evening.

If there's anyone still out there, please listen carefully . . .

TIFFANY FLUFFIT

Billionaire mad scientist
DR. RUPERT MARMALADE
has unleashed an army of
zombie kittens—
commonly known as
ZITTENS ...

MARMALADE: THE FACE OF EVIL

and
NO ONE IS SAFE!

CRASH!

Even this television station has been **SURROUNDED**. I'm not sure how much longer we'll be on the air, but I'll tell you what we know . . .

The Zittens are furry and super-cute but **ABSOLUTELY DEADLY**.

Make no mistake, they will **TRY TO EAT YOU!** But here are a few things that may help you escape . . .

TOP TIPS FOR SURVIVING THE KITTEN APOCALYPSE

First, many of them wear **LITTLE BELLS**. IF YOU HEAR A CUTE LITTLE BELL—

RUN AND HIDE!

Second, they **DO NOT LIKE WATER**. Water is your best **DEFENSE**. It really annoys them and can sometimes make them go away.

And finally, they are easily distracted by **BALLS OF YARN**. If you come across a Zitten, tossing them a ball of yarn is your best chance of **ESCAPE**.

However, if you encounter a **WHOLE LITTER OF ZITTENS**, none of this will help you.

THIS ISN'T GOOD!

If you are attacked by a litter, there is only one thing you can do—

RUN AS FAST AS YOU CAN!

CRASH!

Oh no! They're inside!

MEEEEOOORGWW!

· CHAPTER 1 ·
NOT GOOD

GUYS?

Just
remember—
it could be
worse . . .

WORSE?!

OK, that's it. I say we throw them the wolf so the rest of us can make a run for it.

Stop moving around! You're making the water splash out of the kiddie pool!

Yeah, cut it out, Mr. Snake! That water is the only thing between us and those tiny flesh-eating monsters!

Well, *you'd* know all about **TINY FLESH-EATING MONSTERS**, wouldn't you?

Like you can talk, **MR. I-EAT-MICE-AND-ANY-OTHER-CUTE-LITTLE-FAMILY-PETS!**

We *can't* run away, *hermano*.
We're surrounded.

And maybe that's a
GOOD thing!

WHAT?!

Well . . . this gives us another chance to be awesome, doesn't it?

OK. I've changed my mind. Let's throw them the wolf.

No, no, listen! **DR. MARMALADE**, that rotten little billionaire guinea pig, created this army of Zittens for one reason and one reason only . . .

What reason?

So that we can defeat them and say **"IN YOUR FACE, DR. MARMALADE!"**

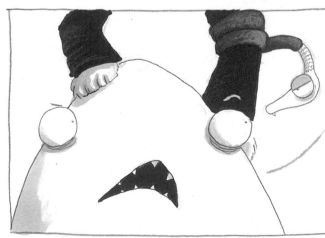

Actually, you know what, guys? I'm with you. Let's throw them the wolf.

No, wait!
I think I hear
something . . .

Don't try to
protect him.
Mr. Wolf needs to
"go be a hero" one
last time . . .

Hush up, Slimy.
What do you hear, Legs?

It sounds like . . .

Like what?

. . . like . . .

LIKE WHAT?!

Does it sound like the claws of a zombie kitten *poking a hole in our kiddie pool*?!

No. It sounds more like . . .

A JET!

It's Agent Fox!

Nice to see you, gentlemen. Climb aboard!

She saved us again!

Yeah. Saved by a girl. *Twice*. This is getting embarrassing.

Embarrassing?! What's wrong with you, *chico*? We're lucky to know such a strong, powerful *señorita*!

Yes. We. Are . . .

Oh, pleassssse . . .

Oh. One small thing, Mr. Wolf . . .

Anything!

Would you mind grabbing one of those Zittens for me? That'd be marvelous.

Oh. Uhhhhh . . . sure.

Um . . . OK.

Here, kitty, kitty, kitty.

Anything for you, Agent Fox . . .

RRREEOOOWW!

POUNCE!

Uh-oh.

Did he get one, Mr. Piranha?

EEEEEEEEE

Ah, yes, *señorita*. I think he's just calming it down with a . . . cuddle.

· CHAPTER 2 ·
TWO PLACES AT ONCE

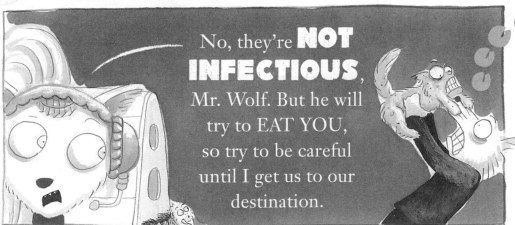

Gentlemen, I know someone who might
be able to help with this Zitten situation.
Her name is

GRANNY GUMBO,

and if we can bring her a live Zitten,
there's a chance she can create an

ANTIDOTE

and turn them all
back into
normal kittens.

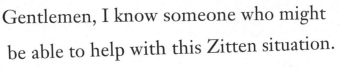

I need to get this Zitten to **GRANNY GUMBO**.

But I *also* need to keep following

DR. MARMALADE.

Trouble is—I can't be
in two places at once.
So, Mr. Shark?
And Mr. Piranha?

Yeah?

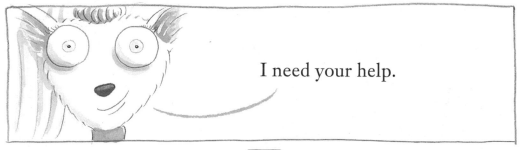

I need your help.

Why us?

Because you two can **SWIM**.

I've managed to track Marmalade to an island

fifty miles off the coast of **COSTA RICA**.

I need you to swim out there, in secret,

and keep an eye on him.

And I hope you don't mind,

but I would recommend

wearing a **DISGUISE**.

Mind? You just made my day. I'm in.

Um . . .

Mr. Piranha? You seem troubled. Is everything OK?

Uh, I might have a slight problem, *señorita* . . .

What?

I'm a freshwater fish.

So?

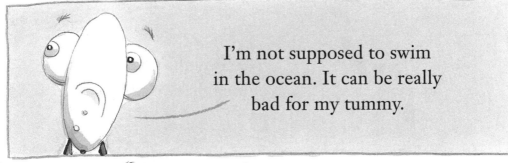

I'm not supposed to swim in the ocean. It can be really bad for my tummy.

Are you kidding?! What is the point of a fish that won't go in the water?

So, let me get this straight—you and
Moby Dick over here *WALK AROUND* like
it's the most normal thing in the world,
but you're worried about getting

A LITTLE SALT IN
YOUR GILLS?!

Hmm, I was actually
wondering how you
manage to walk around
so much myself . . .

. . . not that it's any of
my business . . .

Don't worry, Piranha.
I'll get you to that island
safely. And just for the
record—if we want to
walk around . . .

THAT'S IT!
I'M GONNA EAT THAT UGLY SON OF A CATERPILLAR!

Heeeey! Take it easy, fellas. Agent Fox can hear you. Try to be a little bit cool, will **YOU—**

—ooooohhhhh, my face! It's. Got. My. Face!

Yeah. Sure, Wolf. We'll try to be cool. Just like you.

EEEEEE

Legs? Take us lower.
Mr. Shark? This is your stop.
And Mr. Piranha?
It's your choice . . .

I'll do it, *señorita*. You can count on me.
That guinea pig won't get away from us!

Good for you, Piranha. I'll be thinking of you. And I sure hope you don't get a-**SALT**-ed!

39

Sure. He's an idiot.
But he's *our* idiot.

· CHAPTER 3 ·
GRANNY

This is **GRANNY GUMBO'S WAREHOUSE**. Now, I should warn you— Granny is a *little* bit . . . odd. So you might want to leave the talking to me . . .

Yeah, yeah, whatevs. Hey, look, it's open . . . YO! OLD LADY! WHERE'S THE MILK AND COOKIES?

GRAB!

Well, look what's makin' a ruckus in my parlor! A sweet, tasty

GRUB!

Yumitty YUM YUM YUM! I'm gonna eat you UP!

Oh dear . . .

Oh, you sure are gonna taste goo . . .

goo . . . gaah . . . gAAAH . . .

AAAAHHH...

AAAAAA
AHHHHH...

GRAB!

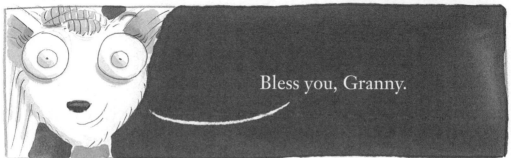

Bless you, Granny.

Who's *that*?
Is that you,
Miss Fox?
I do declare!

But what are you doin' bringing a flea-bitten **MUTT-DOG** into my parlor?! You know I'm allergic to mutt-dogs!

I do apologize, Granny. But I was rather hoping . . .

Oh, never you mind, 'cause you brought me a sweet treat, too!

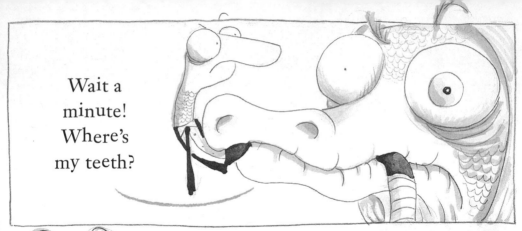

I've got my special brew cookin' right now, as a matter of fact . . .

Marvelous, Granny.

Now, I just need a pinch of his **FUR** . . .

SPRINKLE!
SPRINKLE!

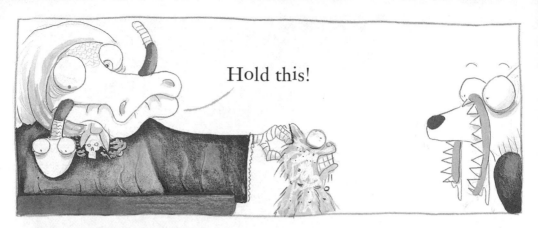

Hold this!

Trouble is . . .

EEEEEEEE

CHOMP!

. . . to finish
my antidote,
I need a squirt of
**SNAKE
BITE
VENOM!**

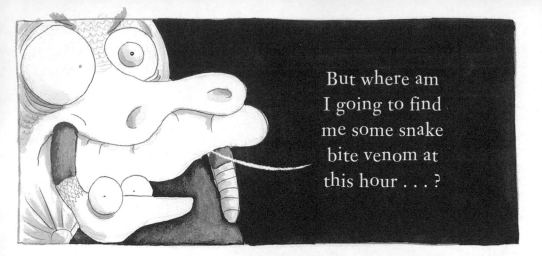

But where am
I going to find
me some snake
bite venom at
this hour . . . ?

Well . . .

Wolf! Don't
you dare . . .

Hush your mouth, Grub.
What's that you're sayin',
Mutt-Dog?

I think you'll find all the venom you need right there in that . . . grub, Granny.

Well, I do declare! I believe you're right—this mean-eyed, low-down snake in the grass will do *nicely* . . .

Now you listen to me—

HUSH, child. And hold still.

Wait a minute, lady. *Have you been professionally trained by a vet to extract venom?!*

· CHAPTER 4 ·
the MASTER OF DISGUISE

OK. Open your eyes . . .

Uhhh . . .
OK. I give up.
Why are you dressed
like a unicorn?

What?! Oh. Sorry. Hang on . . .
Let me change the angle . . .

TA-
DA!

Ohhhhhh! I get it!
You're a **DOLPHIN!**
Man, you are SO good
at disguises.

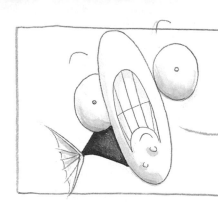

No, no, no, no!
Why are you **NAKED**, *chico*?!

When was the last
time you saw a dolphin
wearing clothes?

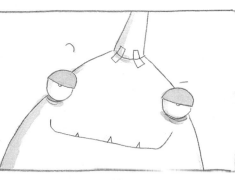

Well . . . never.
But you've been spending
too much time with
that bare-butt spider,

LEGS,

that's what *I* think . . .

Because THIS little dolphin has a pet goldfish named Mindy.

I hope you're not saying what I think you're saying . . .

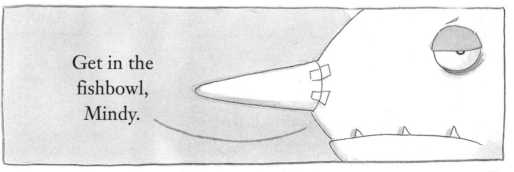

Get in the fishbowl, Mindy.

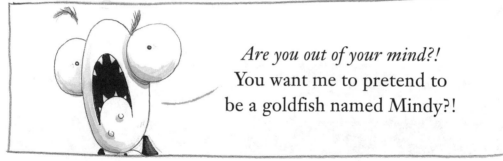

Are you out of your mind?! You want me to pretend to be a goldfish named Mindy?!

Now you're getting it.
When I'm finished with you, **NO ONE**
will recognize us. We'll find Marmalade, and
YOU won't get a drop of salt water on you.

I refuse to be naked,
chico! I won't do it!

Calm down and
put this on. We're
running out of time.

MOMENTS LATER . . .

Don't you ever question one of my disguises again.

Never, *hermano*. I swear. Never again.

· CHAPTER 5 ·
the ANTIDOTE

Wha . . . ?

What happened?

Hello, Mr. Snake. I'm glad to see you're feeling better. It was very kind of you to donate some venom. Granny really appreciates it.

DONATE?! She just **CLOBBERED** me with a frying pan! She's completely *insane*!

Whoa, there! Take it easy, good buddy. I'm sure Agent Fox knows what she's doing . . .

Oh, well, if YOU say so, you **LOVE-STRUCK BUFFOON**, then it MUST be true!

Actually, perhaps we could get Granny to clobber him just one more time, *heh heh heh . . .*

I must apologize for Granny. Her methods are **HIGHLY UNUSUAL**, but I promise you, Mr. Snake— she is a genius.

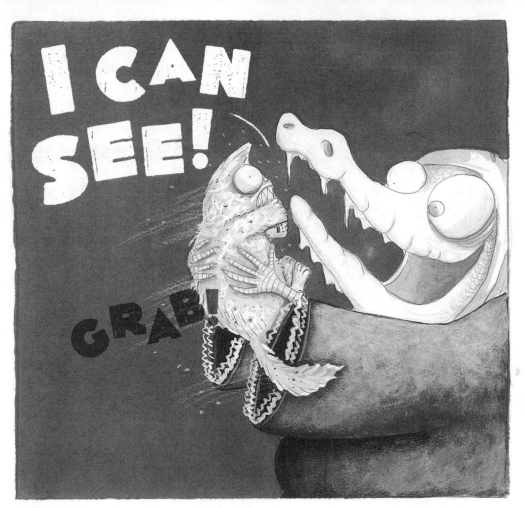

 Oh yeah. She's a genius, all right.

Hush your mouth, Grub, and pass me one of them balls of yarn. It's time for the Granny Gumbo Show!

Wow! Why do you have so much yarn, Granny?

I make it from the hair of all the mutt-dogs I **EAT**.

I thought you were allergic to . . . mutt-dogs . . .

Yeah, but they taste so GOOD, I can't help myself.

Oh no! Zittens!
We're surrounded!

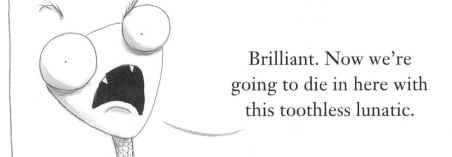

Brilliant. Now we're going to die in here with this toothless lunatic.

Hold it together, gentlemen. Granny? It's time . . .

I hear you! Mutt-Dog, **CATCH!**

Oh my stars! It actually works!

You *are* a genius, Granny!

FART!

What did you say?

I'm sorry to poop on your party, but if we walk out there, those things will tear us to pieces before we toss even one ball of wool. There's just

TOO MANY OF THEM . . .

· CHAPTER 6 ·
TROUBLE ON GUINEA PIG ISLAND

Here's the island, guys!
Isn't it *awesome?*

Wow. These dolphins
are so cute and friendly!

Yeah.

I still feel weird that they're all nude, though. We don't do skinny-dipping in Bolivia, *hermano*.

I know. It's an ocean thing. You'll get used to it. Can you see anything yet?

No, *chico*. I'm worried we're too late. It looks totally deserted. Maybe he . . . wait a minute . . .

LOOK!

MARMALADE!

What's he doing up there?
That looks like a . . .

Hey, guys!
Let's play a game!

Yeah!
Let's see who
can jump the
highest!

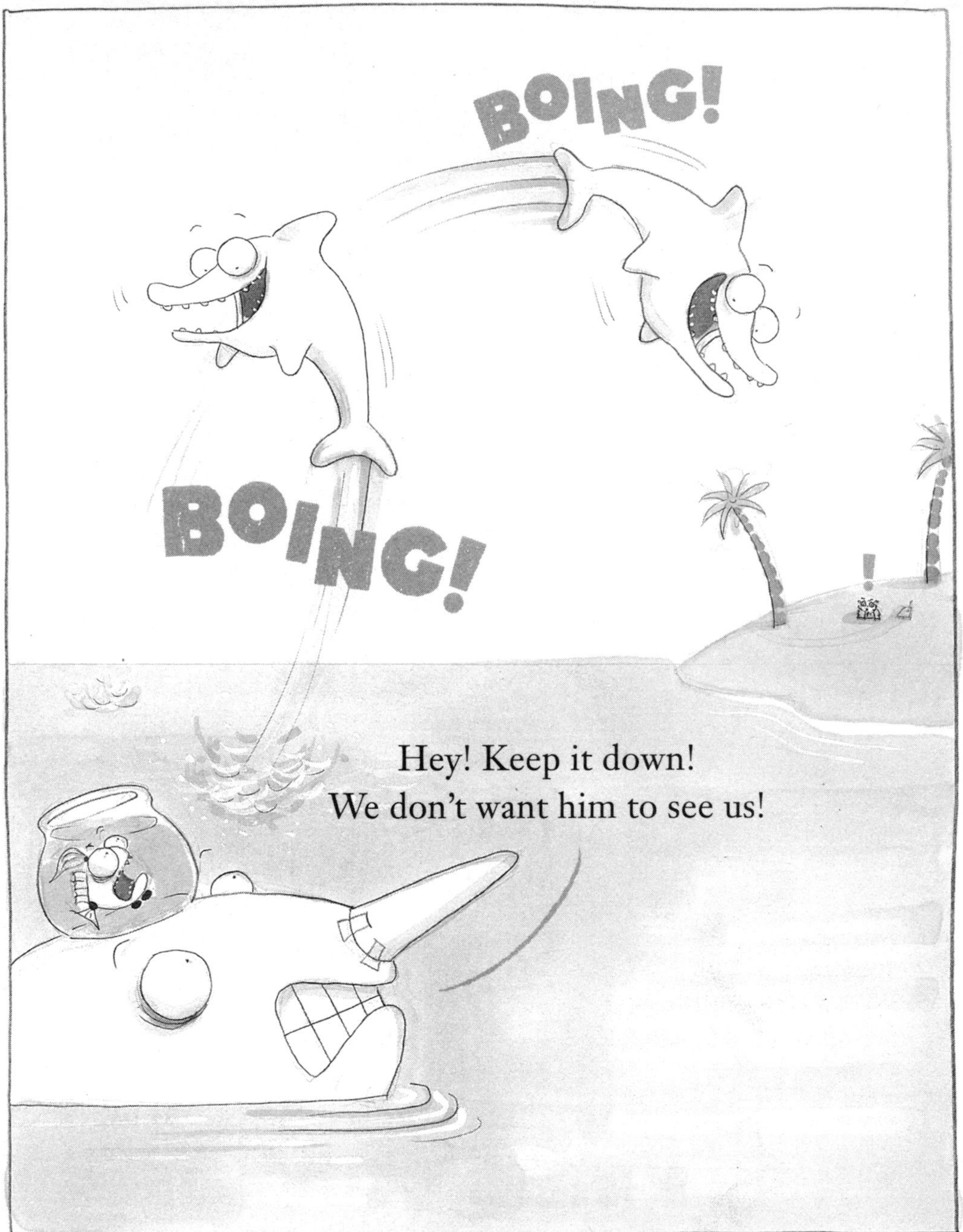
BOING!
BOING!
!
Hey! Keep it down!
We don't want him to see us!

I can't see him. This isn't good.

Man, I thought dolphins were supposed to be smart . . .

That's just a myth. Some of them are really stupid.

I love jumping!

Let's jump some more!

So what do we do now? Should we go up there and look for him?

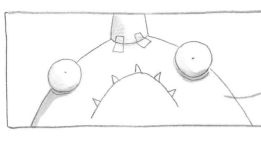

Uh-oh. Somehow I don't think we need to . . .

BOoO OM!

¡Ay, caramba!

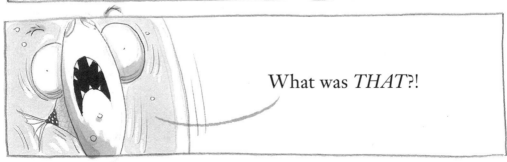

What was *THAT*?!

So where do
you suppose
he's going . . . ?

CHAPTER 7

KEEP ON TRUCKIN'

RANNY GUMBO'S
LL-NATURAL HERBS & POTIONS

OK, gentlemen.
Are we ready to go?

Nearly! I just need to
tighten these pillows . . .

What are you doing, Wolf?

We're GOOD GUYS, remember? We don't want to HURT any kittens. We want to **SAVE** all the kittens.

These **CUSHIONS** and **PILLOWS** will make sure that none of them gets hurt . . . as we plow through them at high speed.

Yeah.

That's the stupidest thing I've ever heard. You've made a perfectly cool truck look ridiculous.

That's just one snake's opinion. I think it looks great.

If by "great" you mean "dumb," then yes—it looks "great."

Quit your yappin' and get up here! It's time to hit the road!

Remember, boys— I'll **DRIVE THE TRUCK**, you **THROW THE YARN**. There are **THOUSANDS** of Zittens so this isn't going to be easy, but if anyone can do it, we can.

You're so awesome! I mean . . . I just love you . . . I mean . . . I think you're the coolest . . . I mean . . . yeah . . . no . . . yeah.

And the winner of the most embarrassing speech award goes to . . .

Don't listen to him, Mr. Wolf. I think you're **GREAT.**

OK, boys. Let's roll . . .

Boys? Can you hear me?

Yes, Agent Fox. What can we do for you?

The Zittens are spread out wider than we thought. We need to find a way to **THROW THE YARN FARTHER**.

Oh yeah?
And how do
you suggest
we do that?

Don't worry,
Agent Fox.
I'll think of
something.
You look lovely
today,
by the way . . .

Thank you,
Mr. Wolf.

Oh **BARF!**

WOLF AND FOX!
SITTING IN A TREE!
K! I! S-S! I-N-G!

Shhh!

STUFF!

Wait a minute.
That gives me . . .

. . . an
IDEA!

VOOOOOOM!

That's IT! Whatever you're doing, Mr. Wolf, keep it up!

Oh, no you don't! You're not going to use me as a

CATAPULT

again! I forbid it! I—

STUFF! STUFF! STUFF!

Nonsense! This is your moment to **SHINE**, little buddy.

The question is—how many balls of yarn does it take to stuff a snake?

Quite a few,
as it turns out.

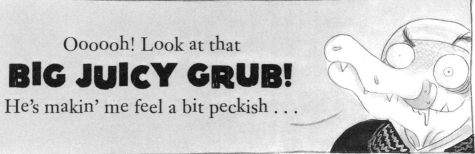

Oooooh! Look at that
BIG JUICY GRUB!
He's makin' me feel a bit peckish . . .

Hey, kitties . . .

That's brilliant, Mr. Wolf!
YOU'VE DONE IT!

WOO-HOO!
NOTHING can stop us now!

Hmmm . . .

MUNCH!

I'm **HUNGRY**, that's what. And I'm fixin' to eat me some **MUTT-DOG**, tooooo . . .

ooo . . .
oooh . . .
ahh . . .
AHHHH . . .

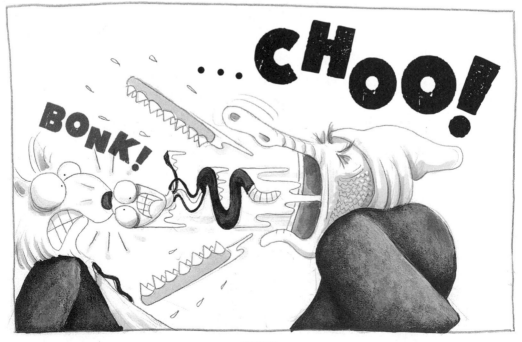

BONK!

. . . CHOO!

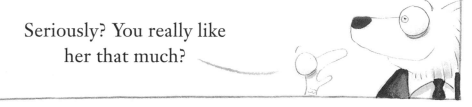

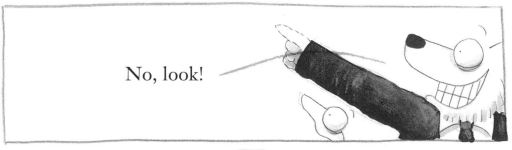

AGENT FOX!

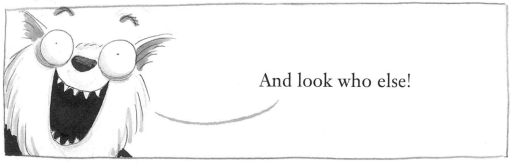

And look who else!

119

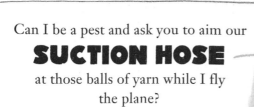 Can I be a pest and ask you to aim our **SUCTION HOSE** at those balls of yarn while I fly the plane?

 Sounds good to me!

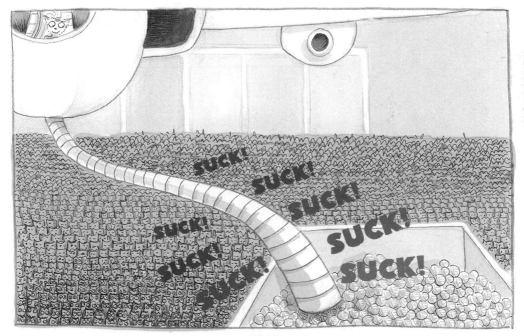

SUCK! SUCK! SUCK! SUCK! SUCK! SUCK! SUCK! SUCK! SUCK!

OK, that should do it. Now . . . let's put a stop to this nonsense, shall we?

You didn't *really* think it would be THAT easy, did you?

SALE! SALE! SALE! SALE! SALE! SALE! SALE!

SHOPPING C

MARMALADE!

• CHAPTER 8 •
the BAD PENNY

Hi, everybody!

Listen carefully because I have a special, private message— just for **YOU!** Aren't you lucky? First of all, congratulations on surviving **PHASE ONE** of my little plan.

Phase One?! I don't like the sound of this . . .

SHOPPING CE

SALE! SALE! SALE! SALE! SALE! SALE! SALE! SALE!

Sure, a few kittens is one thing.
But imagine if I had a weapon SO powerful that it
could turn **EVERY CUTE AND CUDDLY CREATURE ON THE PLANET** into a **DROOLING WEAPON OF DESTRUCTION!**
Wouldn't that just be **AWESOME?!**

He's lying! He doesn't have a weapon like that! That's impossible . . .

Is it? Well, let me introduce you to the CUTE-ZILLA RAY, Mr. Wolf!

CUTE-ZILLA™

Just imagine a world where every puppy . . .

bunny . . .

pony . . .

and dolphin . . .

CUTE-ZILLA™

. . . could be changed,
just by pulling one
little lever . . .

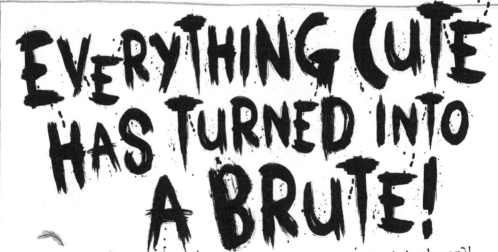

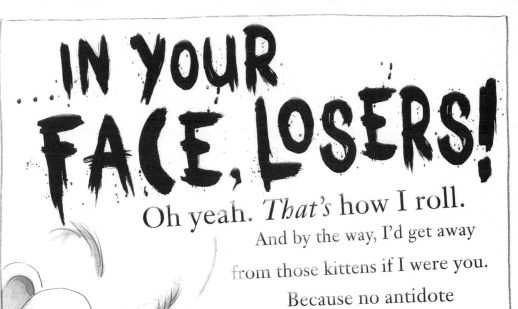

Oh yeah. *That's* how I roll.
And by the way, I'd get away from those kittens if I were you. Because no antidote **ON EARTH** will help you this time . . .

· CHAPTER 9 ·
A BIT FARTHER
THAN EXPECTED

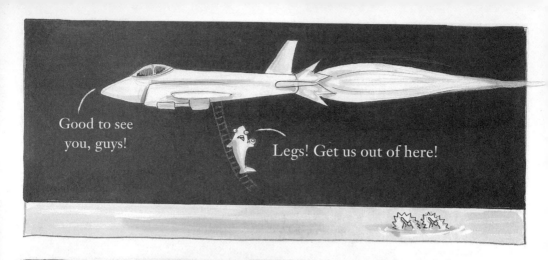

We know.
Nice bikini, by the way.

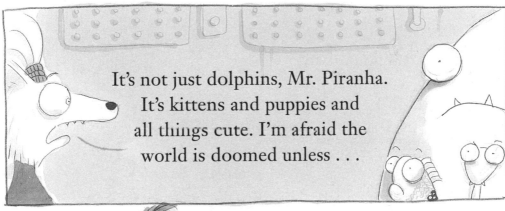

It's not just dolphins, Mr. Piranha.
It's kittens and puppies and
all things cute. I'm afraid the
world is doomed unless . . .

. . . UNLESS WE

SAVE IT.

But how?
We don't even know where the
CUTE-ZILLA RAY is.

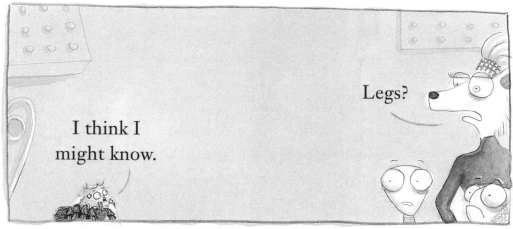

Legs?

I think I
might know.

Well, the only way he'd
be able to use it over the

**WHOLE
PLANET**

is if he's beaming
it in from

SPACE . . .

Where? Where do
we have to get?

Mr. Piranha, we have to get to . . .

THE BAD NEWS? The world is ending.

THE GOOD NEWS?

The **BAD GUYS** are back to **save it!**

Sure, they might have to "borrow" a **rocket** . . .

And there might be something **NASTY** in one

of the **space suits** . . . And Mr Piranha *miiiiight*

have eaten too many **bean burritos** . . .

But seriously, how **BAD** can it be?

How bad?! **SUPER BAD**. It's one small

step for the **Sort-of-International-League-**
of-Good-Guys guys.

It's one giant leap for

the **BAD GUYS** *in*

Intergalactic Gas!